First published in Belgium and Holland by Clavis Uitgeverij, Hasselt – Amsterdam, 2015
Copyright © 2015, Clavis Uitgeverij

English translation from the Dutch by Clavis Publishing Inc. New York
Copyright © 2016 for the English language edition: Clavis Publishing Inc. New York

Visit us on the web at www.clavisbooks.com

*Who Will Dance with Little Mouse?* written and illustrated by Anita Bijsterbosch
Original title: *Muisje wil dansen*
Translated from the Dutch by Clavis Publishing

ISBN 978-1-60537-267-9

This book was printed in January 2016 at Publikum d.o.o., Slavka Rodica 6, Belgrade, Serbia

First Edition
10 9 8 7 6 5 4 3 2 1

Clavis Publishing supports the First Amendment and celebrates the right to read

# Who Will Dance with Little Mouse?

Anita Bijsterbosch

Clavis

**NEW YORK**

Little Mouse loves to dance.
If he could, he'd dance all day long.

"Who will dance with me,
who will dance with me?"

Little Mouse sings.

"Sheep, Sheep,
will you dance with me?"
Little Mouse asks.

"Baa, baa," Little Sheep bleats.
"No, I'd rather jump around.
Look how high I can go!"

"Sloth, Sloth,
will you dance with me?"
Little Mouse asks.

"I'm sorry, Little Mouse, today I just want to hang on a tree with my baby," Sloth says slowly.

"Frog, Frog, do you want to dance with me?" Little Mouse asks.

"Ribbit, ribbit," Frog croaks.
"Not really, I'd rather swim a few laps.
Look how fast I can go."

"Koalas, Koalas,
will you dance with me?"
Little Mouse asks.

"No, Little Mouse.
We're climbing trees today,"
Mommy Koala replies.

"Snail, Snail, will you dance with me?" Little Mouse asks.

"Dance?" Snail asks.
"Let me think about that....
No, I'd rather not.
Today, I just want to glide."

"Puppy, Puppy,
will you dance with me?"
Little Mouse asks.

"Woof, woof," Puppy barks.
"No. I'm going for a long run!
Look how fast I can go!"

"Heron, Heron,
will you dance with me?"
Little Mouse asks.

"No, of course not.
I'm busy standing on one leg,"
Heron grumbles.

Little Mouse can also stand on one leg!
Isn't that great?

"Elephant, Elephant,
will you dance with me?"
Little Mouse asks.

"Barrrraaaagh," Elephant trumpets.
"No, Little Mouse.
I've planned a long walk today.
Look how hard I can stomp."

"Nightingale, Nightingale,
will you dance with me?"
Little Mouse asks.

But Nightingale doesn't answer.
He is singing a pretty song.

"No one wants to dance with me,"
Little Mouse sighs,
"and dancing by myself is no fun."

"I will dance with you!"
a little owl says suddenly.

Little Mouse and Little Owl dance
like they've never danced before.

And look!
More and more animals
are dancing along with them.

Every night Nightingale sings the most beautiful songs.
Especially for everyone who loves to dance,
just like Little Mouse does.